P9-DGU-962

Monster Boy's First Day of School

BY CARL EMERSON
ILLUSTRATED BY LON LEVIN

visit us at www.abdopublishing.com

Published by Magic Wagon, a division of the ABDO Publishing Group, 8000 West 78th Street, Edina, Minnesota 55439.

Printed in the United States.

Text by Carl Emerson
Illustrations by Lon Levin
Edited by Patricia Stockland
Interior layout and design by Emily Love
Cover design by Emily Love

Library of Congress Cataloging-in-Publication Data

Emerson, Carl.
Monster Boy's first day of school / by Carl Emerson ; illustrated by Lon Levin.
p. cm.— (Monster Boy)
ISBN 978-1-60270-237-0
[1. Monsters—Fiction. 2. First day of school—Fiction.] I. Levin, Lon, ill. II. Title.
PZ7.E582Moh 2008
[E]—dc22

2008003651

Mr. and Mrs. Onster stared down at their new baby, Marty. He cooed softly at them.

“What was that horrible noise?” Mrs. Onster blurted out. “It sounded almost human!”

"Monte, I'm worried," Mrs. Onster said to her husband. "Do you think he's a monster, like us?"

"I don't know, Martha," Mr. Onster said. "We probably won't know until he's older. Until then, all we can do is hope."

"And if he is human," Mrs. Onster said, "we will love him no matter what."

Mr. and Mrs. Onster did everything they could to help Marty grow into a snorty, snarly monster.

They filled his bottle with sludge. They taught him to growl, howl, and scratch. They bathed him in slime, combed his hair with a fork, and brushed his teeth with goo.

Still, Marty looked very much like a little boy.

Years passed and not much changed. When Marty's teeth grew long enough to poke out of his mouth, they didn't notice. Even the slobber didn't make them happy.

"Oh, if only he would turn blue," Mrs. Onster said.

Finally, it came time for Marty to begin school.

"Oh dear," Mrs. Onster said worriedly. "What if he fits in? What if no one thinks he is the tiniest bit strange or scary?"

Mr. Onster shivered. "The thought makes my skin uncrawl," he said. "Surely they will run away from him in fear."

But the Onsters knew Marty was far too nice, too human, to scare any of the other children.

Marty headed off for school just like the other boys and girls in his neighborhood. In his backpack he carried everything he would need for the first day.

He had pencils, crayons, and notebooks. He also had a sack lunch. It included a leech sandwich, toenail chips, and scum pudding. He was set to go.

At the school, Marty met all the other children in his class. Many were nice. But one boy, Bart Ully, started picking on Marty right away.

"Hey there, Big Ears," Bart said to Marty.

Marty tried to be nice. "Hi, my name is Marty," he said.

"I like 'Big Ears' better," Bart said. "I'm sticking with that."

Bart didn't stick with "Big Ears." Later that day, he called Marty "Bucky" and "Slobbertooth." But Marty stayed calm. He did not growl. He did not snarl. He simply walked away.

Other kids were nicer to Marty. He made fast friends with Sally Weet. She was very kind.

"Just ignore Bart," Sally would say. "He's a monster."

When Marty returned home from school, he told his parents about his first day.

"This one boy, Bart, was not very nice," Marty said. "He called me all sorts of names."

"EAT HIM!!!" Marty's parents cried out. But Marty didn't think that was the right thing to do. He didn't want to eat anyone. He just wanted to be a regular kid.

Marty spent most of his free time at school with Sally. They did their best to stay away from Bart. But one day, Sally arrived at school wearing a new pair of glasses.

“Nice goggles, Four Eyes!” Bart barked. “Hey, everybody, come check out Sally! Can you see the moon with those telescopes?”

At that moment, something changed inside Marty. His insides felt like they turned upside down. His eyes felt hot. His skin felt thick.

Marty wasn't sure what happened next. Chairs flew. Dust rose. Howls and growls and slobber and snot filled the air.

When it was over, Bart suddenly looked very small. But no one was looking at Bart. All eyes were on Marty. He stood in the center of the room, panting.

Marty knew he did not want to eat Bart. But to everyone else, it looked like he did.

Marty's teacher, Miss Taken, told Marty she was very disappointed and was going to have to call his parents.

She turned to the board and wrote the names of the three students whose parents would have to be called.

B.Ully
M.Onster
S.Weet
STUDENT REPOR

For the first time, Marty noticed what his name looked like. Monster.

The other kids noticed, too.

"Monster! Monster! Marty is a monster!" they cried.

With each chant, Marty grew smaller and smaller. Soon, he was just regular Marty again.

The next day, all of the parents came to meet with Miss Taken. She explained everything that happened.

Mr. and Mrs. Ully were very unhappy with Bart. Mr. and Mrs. Weet were very nice about everything.

"Thank you for sticking up for Sally," Mrs. Weet said to Marty. "I'm sure you wouldn't know, but it's very hard to have something about you that is different from the other children."

Marty tried not to smile.

On the way home, Marty's parents beamed with pride.

"Did you see how frightened the Ully family was?" Mr. Onster asked.

"Yes, I did," Mrs. Onster said. "Oh, Marty, we are so proud of you."

Then Marty's parents offered one final piece of advice to their little monster: "Next time, eat him!"

Contain Your Inner Monster

Tips from Marty Onster

- Tell a teacher if someone is bullying you.
- Take deep breaths to calm down when you are upset.
- No matter what, don't eat people.
- Talk to an adult about what you are feeling.